Sixty at a Blow

Sixty

A TALL TALE

at a Blow

FROM TURKEY

Retold and Illustrated by
Christine Price

E. P. DUTTON & CO., INC. NEW YORK

Library of Congress Catalog Card Number: 68-16253

First Edition

Grateful acknowledgment is made to George G. Harrap & Company, Ltd. (London) for permission to retell this story which was
first published in 1913 in their book *Forty-Four Turkish Fairy
Tales* translated and collected by Ignacz Kunos.

For
Nargis Fazl

Once there was

and once there was not, a man named Kara Mustafa, who was so timid he dared not go out alone. He did not even like to be left alone in the house when his wife went to visit her friends.

His wife was most annoyed with him. She tried to cure her husband of his fear by slipping away and leaving him alone in the street when they were out together one evening. But this did no good at all. Mustafa was more frightened than ever. The next day his wife mocked him and called him a coward; and at that, Mustafa flew into such a rage that he decided to leave her then and there.

So he took an old rusty knife that had belonged to his father, stuck it in the sash around his middle, and set out to seek his fortune.

He had only just started down the street when he almost stepped in a sticky pool of spilled honey, covered with a swarm of flies. Still seething with rage, Mustafa swept his knife across the crowd of flies, and killed sixty of them at a blow. When he attacked them a second time, his score was seventy.

This gave him an idea. He hurried to the bazaar to find the shop of the cutler, who made knife-blades, and he ordered the cutler to engrave an inscription on the old knife: "At a single blow Kara Mustafa, the great hero, has killed sixty, and at the second blow, seventy."

And when the inscription was done, Mustafa set out again to seek his fortune.

Soon he had left the town behind and was walking through wild and lonely places. At nightfall, he lay down and slept among the rocks, sticking his knife into the earth beside him.

Now in that wilderness there lived a band of forty giants. One of them was taking an early walk next morning and saw Mustafa asleep with the knife at his side. The giant bent down and read

the inscription on the knife, and he was seized
with terror. He decided it would be very wise to

make friends with a hero who could kill sixty at a blow. So he waited until Mustafa stirred and began to wake, and then gave him a polite greeting and begged him to join the giants' company.

When Mustafa opened his eyes and saw the giant bending over him, his hair and moustache stood on end, and he prayed he might still be dreaming.

"Who are you?" he gasped at last.

"We are a band of forty giants," said the giant humbly. "And if you will deign to join us, we shall be forty-one."

Mustafa began to breathe again and to twirl his moustache. "I am willing," he said. "Go and tell the others."

Hearing this, the giant hastened away to his fellows. "My brothers," he said, "a hero desires to join us. His immense strength may be gathered from the inscription on his knife: 'At a single blow Kara Mustafa, the great hero, has killed sixty, and at the second blow, seventy.' Let us put everything in order, for he will be here directly."

So the giants all hastened to meet Mustafa.

When he saw them he felt his courage sink. However, he managed to address them. "God greet you, comrades!"

The giants modestly returned his greeting, and offered him a place among them. Mustafa twirled his moustache and looked them over. "Is there among you," he said, "a fellow like me — a slayer of sixty at a blow?"

The giants shook their heads.

"If there had been such a man," said Mustafa, deeply relieved that there was not, "I should

have challenged him to step forward and try his
strength with me."

"Where could we ever find your equal?" ex-
claimed the frightened giants.

Now the giants were obliged to carry water to their houses from a well a long distance away, and this duty was performed in turn by each of them. Being of gigantic stature and enormous strength, they were able to carry a quantity of water impossible for a mere mortal.

The day after Mustafa joined them, one of the giants said to him humbly, "I fear it is your turn to fetch the water, and we are sorry that the well is so far away."

Mustafa considered for a moment, twirling his moustache, and then asked for a rope. They gave him one, and he strode off to the well with the rope on his shoulder. The giants looked on from a distance, full of curiosity to see what he would do. When they saw him tie the rope firmly around the stonework of the well, they rushed over and demanded to know what he was up to.

"Oh," he answered, "I am only going to put the well on my back and bring it home, so that none of us need to go so far to fetch water again!"

18

They begged him, for Allah's sake, not to do such a thing, and he promised not to, if they would trouble him no more with the duty of water-carrying.

A few days later, it was Mustafa's turn to fetch wood from the forest. Again he asked for the rope, and the giants hid themselves and watched him. On the edge of the forest they saw him drive a peg into the ground and fix the rope to it. Then he passed the rope around all the tree trunks, and just as he drew it tight a wind came up and shook the trees.

"What are you doing, Mustafa?" shouted one of the giants.

"Oh," said Mustafa, "I am only going to take home the forest all at once, instead of piecemeal, to save trouble."

"Pray don't shake the trees!" shouted all the giants, thoroughly alarmed. "You will destroy the whole forest. We would rather fetch the wood ourselves."

The giants were now more afraid of Mustafa than ever, and they called a council to decide on the best way to get rid of him. They agreed at last to pour boiling water on him during the night while he slept, and thus kill him. Fortunately for Mustafa, however, he overheard their conversation, for it is hard for giants to talk softly.

When evening came, he was well prepared. The giants saw him go to bed in his house as usual. Then they heated an enormous caldron of water, and removing some tiles from the roof of the house, they poured the scalding water down inside.

But in the place where Mustafa should have slept he had laid a bolster with his bedcover drawn over it and his turban rolled up at one end. He himself had settled down in a corner of the room and slept soundly, out of harm's way.

The next day the giants came knocking at his door, believing that Mustafa was dead.

"Who's there?" cried a cheerful voice from inside.

The astonished and frightened giants called to Mustafa to get up as it was already nearly midday. "I had a poor night," he explained, yawning. "It was rather uncomfortably hot, and the sweat poured down me in streams."

The giants were speechless with amazement to find that the boiling water had no more effect on him then to make him sweat!

They were still more determined to kill him now, and they resolved to drop forty iron balls on him while he slept. Fortunately, they again talked so loudly that Mustafa heard them.

When bedtime came, he went into his house and arranged the bolster and turban on the mattress as he had done before. Then he retired to his corner to watch what happened.

The giants mounted the roof, and lifting some of the tiles, looked down on what they thought was their sleeping companion. Mustafa heard them whispering, as softly as they could, "Look, there is his chest; there is his head," and then down came the iron balls—*bang, crash, boom!*—one after the other.

Next morning, when the giants went to Mustafa's house and knocked at the door, no answer came, and they began to congratulate themselves that the hero would trouble them no more. Just to make sure, they knocked again, and shouted. Then their hearts sank, for they heard Mustafa's voice: "Please leave me in peace, my friends. I could not sleep last night for the mice gamboling over me. Pray let me rest a little longer."

The giants were now nearly crazy. What manner of man was this, who thought heavy iron balls were mice?

A few days later the giants hit on a new plan to get rid of Mustafa. "Dear friend," they said, "you must know that in the next province we have a giant-brother who would be delighted to meet you in a trial of strength. Would you consider fighting a duel with him?"

"Is he a strong fellow?" asked Mustafa.

"Very strong."

"Then he may come."

In saying this, however, Mustafa was ready to die of fright. He felt even worse when the gigantic giant appeared on the scene, bigger than all the rest.

29

"Before we fight with swords," said the stranger, in a voice that shook the mountainside and made Mustafa's turban tremble on his head, "let us flex our muscles with a little wrestling bout."

Mustafa nodded his agreement, and they all went forth to an open field. The giant caught Mustafa by the throat at once and held him in such a mighty grip that his eyes started from their sockets.

"What are you staring at?" the giant demanded in surprise, as he relaxed his grip on the hero's neck.

Mustafa got his breath back and answered, still staring at the sky, "I was looking to see how high I should have to throw you so that all your limbs would be broken by your fall."

The giant dropped Mustafa like a hot cake, and all the others fell on their knees and begged the hero to spare their beloved brother. Mustafa consented to call off the duel and to pardon the stranger-giant, and the forty giants entreated him to take a sack of gold pieces and go home. Mustafa graciously accepted the money and expressed his willingness to go, trying not to sound too eager. He gave the whole company a fond farewell, and with the sack of gold on his shoulder, he set out for the town, escorted by one of the giants, who had been ordered to act as his guide.

When he arrived in sight of his home, Mustafa saw his wife looking out of the window. She saw him too, and screamed out for all the neighbors to hear, "Here comes my coward of a husband with a giant!"

Mustafa made a sign to her, behind the giant's back, to say no more, and then ran for the house as fast as he could put foot to the ground.

"Where are you off to?" shouted the giant.

"Into the house to get a bow and arrow to shoot
you!" answered the flying hero, and the giant
turned tail and rushed home to his brothers.

Mustafa hardly had time to rest in his house and tell his wife and neighbors about the forty giants before news came to the town that a fierce bear was playing havoc in the district. The townspeople went to the governor and begged him to order Mustafa the hero to slay the animal.

"It is terrible," they said, "that the bear should be allowed to kill so many poor people. Slaying him will be child's play for Mustafa, the conqueror of forty giants."

The governor sent for Mustafa, and informed him that it was not right that the people should be terrorized by a bear while the province held such a courageous man as himself.

Mustafa twirled his moustache, and quite agreed. "Show me the place where the bear is," he said, "and let forty horsemen go with me."

Forty horsemen were summoned at once, and Mustafa went into the governor's stable, took a handful of pebbles, and flung them among the horses. All the horses began to rear and prance, except for one tired old nag in the corner. This one Mustafa chose for himself.

The forty horsemen, who had been looking on, remarked to the governor that the man was mad and that they had no mind to help him hunt the bear. The governor agreed with them and gave them some quiet advice: "As soon as you hear the bear, go away and leave Mustafa alone with him, to do what he will."

So the cavalcade set out, armed to the teeth
with swords and lances. Away from the town they
rode in fine array, and up the rocky mountainside
where the bear had his den. Soon the mighty
beast heard the clatter of the horses' hooves. He
peered out of the mouth of his den, and at his
first terrible roar the mounted escort whirled
around in a cloud of dust and left Mustafa alone.

41

He spurred his steed, but the poor old horse
would not move, and the bear was charging at
them with long, loping strides. Luckily there was
a tree close by, and Mustafa scrambled to his
feet on the back of the horse and swung himself
into the branches.

Not a minute too soon! The horse swerved out
from under him as the bear came charging up
with a fearful roar and grabbed the tree trunk,

ready to climb after the man. But Mustafa waited no longer. Letting go his hold, he dropped squarely onto the bear's back. Then he boxed the bear's ears so hard that the mighty beast set off at a gallop down the hill after the horsemen, with Mustafa bouncing about on top of him.

Down, down they rushed at whirlwind speed until the hurrying horsemen came in sight at the bottom, and Mustafa yelled to them with all his strength: "Kara Mustafa the hero is coming, the slayer of sixty at a blow!"

They all wheeled around again, just in time for the bear to charge into the midst of them, and in a storm of dust and pounding hooves they killed the bear with their lances.

After this the fame of Kara Mustafa spread far and wide. The governor of the town honored and rewarded him for capturing the bear, and Mustafa was able to rest at last from his adventures. He enjoyed the respect of his neighbors to his long life's end, and as for his wife—she thought him the greatest hero in the world!